Star Crazy

Other titles in the First Young Puffin series

Star Crazy

Written and illustrated by

Valerie Solís

PUFFIN BOOKS

PUFFIN BOOKS

Published by the Penguin Group
Penguin Books Ltd, 27 Wrights Lane, London W8 5TZ, England
Penguin Putnam Inc., 375 Hudson Street, New York, New York 10014, USA
Penguin Books Australia Ltd, Ringwood, Victoria, Australia
Penguin Books Canada Ltd, 10 Alcorn Avenue, Toronto, Ontario, Canada M4V 3B2
Penguin Books (NZ) Ltd, Private Bag 102902, NSMC, Auckland, New Zealand

On the World Wide Web: www.penguin.com

Penguin Books Ltd, Registered Offices: Harmondsworth, Middlesex, England

First published 2000
1 3 5 7 9 10 8 6 4 2

Copyright © Valerie Solís, 2000
All rights reserved

The moral right of the author/illustrator has been asserted

Set in Bembo Schoolbook

Made and printed in Hong Kong by Midas Printing Ltd

British Library Cataloguing in Publication Data
A CIP catalogue record for this book is available from the British Library

ISBN 0–141–30284–4

Go-go the little penguin lived right at
the bottom of the world. He loved his
frozen home. But sometimes he wished
he wasn't a penguin at all!

The problem was that Go-go hated swimming. He couldn't even dive. What he liked was the sky. Go-go knew the names of all the different stars in the sky and which ones were brightest.

"I wish I could fly up to see the stars," he sighed to his mother one night.

"Penguins aren't meant to fly through the air. We fly through the water," laughed his mother. "Why don't you dream about the sea? The sea has its own magic."

But Go-go only wanted to think about the stars. "I wonder what makes them twinkle," he thought, as he drifted off to sleep.

One night, the stars put on an extra-special light show. It was the best Go-go had ever seen. Suddenly a huge ball of light with a long glowing tail appeared. It was a shooting star!

The bright star crossed the sky and vanished from sight.

That night, Go-go couldn't stop thinking about the star. Where had it gone?

Go-go decided he would try to find it.

Go-go woke up early the next morning. He was very excited and told his mother his plan.

"Please be careful, my little Go-go," she said, waving goodbye.

Go-go looked for the star all morning, but it was nowhere to be found. He sat down on an iceberg to think.

All of a sudden, there was a loud
WHOOSH sound. A spout of water flew
into the air! What could it be?

Go-go saw a little whale.

"Hello, I'm Blue," said the whale. "What's your name?"

"I'm Go-go," said Go-go. Then he told Blue all about the fantastic light show and how the star had raced across the sky and disappeared.

"And now I'm looking for the star!" explained Go-go.

"I wish I could see the star too. Can I help you look for it? Perhaps it fell in the sea. We could dive down to the seabed and look there," suggested Blue.

"I'd like to, but I can't dive," admitted Go-go.

"A penguin who can't dive!"exlaimed Blue. "Come on, I'll show you how."

Blue dived down into the water. After
a moment Go-go followed him. It was
easy!

When they reached the seabed, Go-go
couldn't believe his eyes. The fish

sparkled just like stars. Jellyfish flew
through the water like comets in the
night sky.

But Blue nudged Go-go gently.
"Come on, we've got to find the star."

They looked under
rocks and inside
caves. They saw
starfish and
anemones. But they
still couldn't find the
star.

Go-go and Blue
dived deeper and
deeper. As he looked
around, Go-go
thought the sea was
the most magical
thing he had ever
seen.

Suddenly, Go-go noticed a trail of glitter.
"Look, Blue!" he exclaimed. "Perhaps
the glitter comes from the star."

They followed the bright trail along
the seabed until they reached a forest of

kelp. Inside, it was too dark to see.

"Oh dear, we've lost the trail," said Go-go. "What shall we do, Blue?"

Just then a small flashlight fish appeared.

The flashlight fish went inside the kelp
forest and lit the way.

Go-go and Blue smiled at each other
and followed the fish.

At last they found the star, resting
on the bottom of the sea, amid the
ruin of an old shipwreck. It was
caught in a sail.

But the star wasn't sparkly at all. All its glitter had fallen off.

"Why doesn't it sparkle?" asked Go-go sadly.

Blue said, "It needs to be in the sky to sparkle. We'll have to think of a way to take it back up."

"I know, Blue!" Go-go exclaimed.

"We can use the sail to pick up the star and all the glitter. If you could do a big spout, I could take the star up to the sky in the sail."

"I can do a giant spout. I'm the best spouter in whale school," said Blue proudly.

Go-go put the star into the middle of the sail. Then he swept the glitter back into the sail with his wings. Blue helped him with his tail.

Together, Go-go and Blue carried the
sail and the star up to the surface.

Go-go clambered into the sail. Blue
got ready to spout.

WHOOOSH! Up flew Go-go and the
star. Soon they were high in the sky.

The star began to sparkle! Go-go knew it was time to put it back. He threw the star out of the sail into the sky. It stayed there, twinkling with the other stars. Go-go held on tight to the sail, which floated down like a parachute.

Go-go landed gently on Blue's back. Together they looked up at the sky. There, up among all the stars, was a star that shone more brightly than the others.

"Look! There's our star," said Go-go, pointing to the brightest one.

"It's the most beautiful and sparkly one in the sky," Blue replied.

Blue took Go-go back to the shore and they said goodbye.

"What a wonderful time we've had," said Go-go. "Thank you."

Go-go told his mother all about his adventure.

"At last I've been up to the sky. It is very special, but the sea is just as beautiful. And now I love to dive!" said Go-go.

Go-go still dreams about the stars. But he dreams about starfish too.